Black Lagoon® Adventures

SPECIAL EDITION #2:

HUBIE COOL: SUPER SPY

Get more monster-sized laughs from

The Black Lagoon®

Black Lagoon® Adventures
SPECIAL EDITION #2:

HUBIE COOL: SUPER SPY

by Mike Thaler
Illustrated by Jared Lee

SCHOLASTIC INC.

In memory of Alex Wagner, a hero.
—M.T.

To Phil Miller
—J.L.

← HOUSEFLY

Text Copyright © 2016 by Mike Thaler
Illustrations Copyright © 2016 by Jared Lee

ISBN 978-0-545-85076-6

10 9 8 7 6 5 4 3 2   16 17 18 19 20

Printed in the U.S.A.   40
First printing 2016

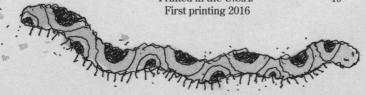

CONTENTS

EGG ⟶

CHAPTER 1
IN THE TICK OF TIME

The dial of the egg timer ticks off the seconds: five, four, three . . . in two seconds the entire world will blow up.

Only one person can save it— Agent Hubie Cool, Double Oh-Oh.

THE DETONATOR HAS BEEN DISCONNECTED!

BIG NASTY BOMB

"Hubie, it's time for bed!"

"I'm busy, Mom."

"Hubie, brush your teeth and it's off to sleep for you."

"But, Mom, I have to save the world."

"Save it tomorrow."

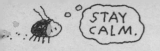

CHAPTER 2
THE BIG SQUEEZE

I go into the bathroom and pick up the toothpaste. The microchip is in the toothpaste tube. I squeeze hard. A large blob of toothpaste lands on my toothbrush. I squeeze again. My toothbrush is now covered with toothpaste.

"Hubie, what on earth are you doing?"

"Looking for a microchip, Mom."

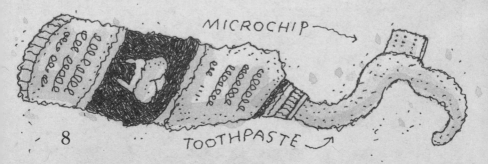

MICROCHIP →

TOOTHPASTE ↗

"I'll give you a chip if you don't stop making a mess and wasting half a tube of toothpaste. Now brush your teeth, put on your pajamas, and get in bed!"

"But Mom—" I say.

"Don't forget to floss because tomorrow we're going to the dentist!"

FLOSS

CHAPTER 3

TO TELL THE TOOTH

"Hubie, it's time to go to the dentist."

"Aw, Mom. My teeth are fine."

"We have a 3:30 appointment and we're going."

TAPEWORM

All secret agents get tortured at one time in their careers, but I get tortured twice a year.

We walk into Dr. Payne's office. More like Mom drags me in. They take me right into the torture chamber. I don't even get to look at the magazines.

Dr. Payne is waiting, gleefully rubbing together his rubber gloves. He's wearing his mask and goggles. He's got a white tray with all his torture tools. They strap me in the torture chair.

13

"Well, Hubie, have we been brushing our teeth?"

I don't know about him, but I have.

"Yes," I answer.

All agents crack under this kind of questioning eventually, but that's all I'm gonna tell him.

"Let's have a look," he smiles.

I clamp my jaws shut.

"Open up, Hubie," he smiles, lifting a crowbar.

He turns on a bright light right in my face, and moves in for the kill.

Secret Agent Double Oh-Oh is a tough bird. I can take a lot of pain as long as it doesn't hurt. It'll be a long time before I crack.

Dr. Payne asks me a lot of questions.

"How's school?"

"How's your mom?"

"How's your dog?"

"Are you in Little League?"

"What's your batting average?"

I don't tell him a thing. I can't . . . his hands are in my mouth.

"Looks like I have to drill," he says.

"I'll talk, I'll talk! I had a candy bar last night. Don't hurt me, don't hurt me!"

"It won't hurt," smiles Dr. Payne . . . and it doesn't.

His first name is "Les."

TOO SCARED
TO MOVE

The candy bar was the only thing I told him about, but I gave him false information. It was an ice cream bar, and I had two. Secret Agent Cool triumphs again and outsmarts the fiendish forces of darkness. And they even give me a new toothbrush and some dental floss.

"I'm cool."

CHAPTER 4
SECRET DREAMS

Secret Agent Cool never gets to rest. Not while there are bad guys out there.

It is dark in the submarine as it nears the foreign shore. I sit in my wet suit. In minutes

I will leave the safety of the submarine and swim ashore. The entire crew looks at me with admiration. Very few would have the courage and stamina to pull this off.

Swimming miles to shore, traveling undercover through the heart of a foreign country. All to gain access to a heavily guarded secret facility and steal the plans to their new, ultimate super weapon.

"Agent Cool. It's time. Are you ready?" the president asks over the radio.

"Ready and steady."

"It's not too late to cancel this

CAN I BORROW YOUR CELL PHONE?

SURE, IT'S IN MY STOMACH.

whole mission. Nobody would blame you."

"Open the hatch, commander. Duty calls."

GOOD LUCK, HUBIE.

THANK YOU, CAPTAIN.

I get out of the bathtub and head into my room.

CHAPTER 5
FINICKY EATERS

I get into my bed and put the covers over my head because I'm an undercover agent.

I slip back into the ocean. The water is cold. The light of the distant shore seems miles away. Then I see the fins. Nobody mentioned sharks. Well, in the spy biz you just have to take whatever comes at you. I hope they don't want to catch a quick bite. I keep swimming. Luckily, they'd already had their bedtime snack. I didn't even have to use my special super shark dental floss.

WHY ARE YOU WEARING LIPSTICK?

I'M A LADYBUG.

23

After swimming for miles, a spotlight hits me.

Mom pops her head into my room. "Hubie, are you still up? It's 10:30 and tomorrow's a school day."

"Busted," I say.

WHAT ARE YOU MUMBLING ABOUT?

BUT, MOM, I'VE REACHED THE SHORE.

CHAPTER 6
CLASSY-FIED

The chief wants to see me. I am excited as I stride down the hall of the Central Intelligence Agency. I walk with confidence. My eyes, ears, and nose are always on alert. That is the life of a super spy.

SUPER
SPIDER

I take in every detail: the click of the combination locks as another agent puts a classified document in his wall safe. The grind of a pencil sharpener as it makes a sharp point on a No. 2 pencil.

I smell fish in the cafeteria. It must be Friday, I realize, as I walk into the main office.

Mrs. Armbender, the chief's assistant, looks up from decoding secret messages.

"The principal will see you now, Hubie."

YUMMY!

I UNDERSTAND.

The chief is in deep cover. I enter his office through a secret door. He is sitting behind his desk poring over classified documents. He has a worried look on his face.

"Hubie, Mrs. Green tells me you've been daydreaming in class again."

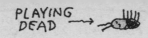

"Yes, Chief."

"I want you to try and concentrate on your class work."

I nod. He means *classified* work. The chief always talks in code. You never know who is listening. He has just given me another dangerous assignment—one where the fate of every man, woman, and child in the world hangs in the balance.

Someone's stealing beans from all over the planet. Navy beans, kidney beans, lima beans, butter beans, Boston beans, garbanzos. There has been a string of bean thefts. The chief wants me to get to the bottom of it, and find the meaning of the beaning.

29

I leave his office with a sense of purpose and dedication. I have a hunch that Dr. Gastro and his international crime organization, P.E.W., are behind it all. But where can I find him? Where do I start?

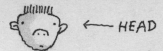 ← HEAD

I head for the library. If anyone can help me, Mrs. Beamster, in research, can.

CHAPTER 8
KNOW YOUR BEANS

She gives me a book of bean riddles. I study it carefully:

What do you call a peaceful bean?
A serene bean.

What do you call a nasty bean?
A mean bean.

What do you call a bean that takes a bath?
A clean bean.

32

What are the smartest beans in the world?
Human beans.

I check out every other bean book in the library. I put on my beanie, and read them all. The only thing I learn is that the bean capital of the world is not Boston, it's Lima, Peru. I guess that's where lima beans come from.* At least now I have a place to start.

* JUST A BAD JOKE

I board the three o'clock flight to Lima. None of the other passengers are aware that their fate hangs on me. Their biggest concern is homework, while mine is saving the nose-zone layer.

CHAPTER 9
PERUSING IN PERU

When I reach Lima, I check into a shady hotel. The lawn needs cutting and there is a dog in the hall. The clerk eyes me suspiciously and the dog wags its tail.

35

"Hubie, are you okay?"

I give her a nod and go to my room. I immediately lock the door and check for bugs. The room is clean except for a pile of underwear in the corner. I quickly put on a disguise. Then I grab my jet-powered spy skateboard and head for the street.

"Hubie, don't be late for dinner," the clerk mumbles as I go out the door.

I start down the street. The dog follows me. He is a P.E.W. agent with a very good disguise. I skate to the harbor.

DISGUISE

TOY BOAT

LOOKOUT

The fishermen are talking about giant green bubbles coming up from the ocean floor. They are afraid to go out onto the water. Two boats have already disappeared. I think I'm on the scent. I rent a rowboat and cast off. The sea is calm.

Suddenly, there's a motion in the ocean. Then it happens! A giant green bubble rises before me and bursts!

Pew! It stinks! I faint. I wake up back in my room. Someone's pounding on the door.

"Time for dinner, Hubie."

I wash my nose and go to the dining room. We're having hot dogs, but the beans are missing. They have been replaced by broccoli. This is more serious than I ever imagined. I know I'll have to return to the ocean to get to the bottom of this. Who knows what evil lurks in the behind of man?

CHAPTER 10
BOTTOM'S UP

That night, I put on my most comfortable flannel wet suit and scuba gear to slip into the ocean.

WHAT'S THAT?

Down and down I go, dimmer, darker, deeper. Then I see it, two metal domes on the ocean floor,

41

rumbling menacingly. A steady stream of little green bubbles are rising from them. I'm sure that inside the dome sits my archenemy, Dr. Gastro, pressing buttons and pulling levers, in his latest stage of toxic *evilution*.

How to get in? I swim around and around the domes. There are no doors. No doorbells. No welcome mats. Then I hear an evil laugh echo in my ears. It's not a laugh, it's an alarm.

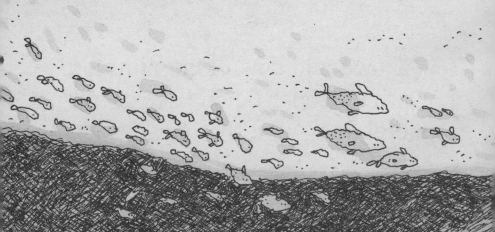

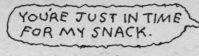

YOU'RE JUST IN TIME FOR MY SNACK.

"Get up, Hubie. It's time for school. Hurry or you'll miss the bus," Mom says while shaking me awake.

I put on my disguise of a third grader. I feel good about discovering the laboratory of Dr. Gastro. I brush my teeth, and think about finishing the job.

HURRY UP, HUBIE!

CHAPTER 11
GASTEROIDS

I climb aboard the yellow diving bell.

As I reach the domes, a door opens and Dr. Gastro greets me.

"I've been expecting you, Hubie, and you're right on time," he smiles. "Let me show you my latest invention."

THERE'S THE DOOR! THERE'S DR. GASTRO!

HUBIE, I PRESUME?

I follow Dr. Gastro downstairs into a room full of weird pipes coming from a huge furnace in the center.

"This," he says proudly, "is my Gasitron." He shovels in another load of beans.

"With it," laughs Dr. Gastro, "I will rule the world. The ozone layer will become the nose-zone slayer."

"You're full of beans," I say.

"Oh yeah," he sneers, "Who is gonna stop me?"

"I'm gonna stop you," I reply.

"Oh yeah, oh yeah? You and who else?"

← BEANS

GAS MASK →

CHAPTER 12
SQUEEZE THE BREEZE

MRS. GREEN.

"Yes, Hubie," says Mrs. Green.

"There is a great threat to the ozone layer," I exclaim.

"What kind of threat, Hubie?" she asks.

"Gas," I answer.

"What kind of gas?" she inquires.

"Natural gas," I mumble.

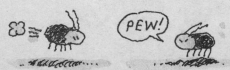

PEW!

"What kind of natural gas?" she persists.

"The kind that I can't mention in public."

Everyone giggles.

FUMES

Well, I'm back on my way to see the chief. This time he doesn't look happy at all.

"Hubie, did you have an outburst in class today?"

"Yes, sir, but I've discovered where all the beans are going."

He folds his hands, and leans closer to me.

"Some things are just not appropriate to discuss in public."

"You mean they're classified— top secret," I say.

He clears his throat, "Yes, Hubie, they're classified and private."

"Got you, Chief," I wink.

WHAT ARE YOU?

A PRIVATE EYE.

MIRAGE ⟶

"Good, Hubie. Now go back to class and don't leak out any more secrets."

I nod and leave his office, but at last I know I'm on the right scent.

CHAPTER 13

IT'S A GAS, MAN

"Boy, Hubie, you were cool in class today."

I turn to Eric. "I can't talk about it," I say. "It's top secret."

"It seemed more like bottom secret to me," laughs Eric.

HA, HA, HA.

52

My friends don't have any idea that I'm a super spy. My cover is perfect. They all think I'm just a kid. It would be too dangerous for them if they knew the truth. I walk away from Eric.

I climb into my spy submarine and decide I'm not coming up until Dr. Gastro is history and his threat is all bottled up.

I NEED A NAP.

STAY ALERT.

As I head down, I see all sorts of fish swimming by the window. The sea is a rainbow of different color fins. Finally, we arrive at my stop. The door opens and I swim out. But the domes are gone. This is not good. Where in the world did Dr. Gastro go? And where will he strike next?

ACCORDING TO THE GPS THE DOMES SHOULD BE RIGHT THERE.

UNBELIEVABLE!

CHAPTER 14
A MAD AD

To relax, I watch my favorite cartoon on television.

But what I see on the screen looks familiar. It's Dr. Gastro in front of the Gasitron. He's broadcasting a threat to the world. Total annihilation if we don't give him ten zillion dollars and season tickets to Yankee Stadium. He says the world has ten days. Then he blips off.

I've got to find him before he carries out his fiendish plan, but where is he? Boston? Chili? The Carib-bean?

I've got to find him before the
world gets twirled.

CHAPTER 15
THE LAST GASP

At dinner, I get my first clue. We're having turkey. That's it!

I catch the sleeper train to Istanbul, Turkey. When I arrive, I check into a small hotel. Then I scour the marketplace. No clues, but lots of rugs. I rent a camel and ride out into the desert. It's hot. I see two domes glistening in the sunlight. But when I ride toward them—they vanish. Was it just a mirage?

Z-Z-Z

WHAT'S THAT?

YOUR EYES CAN DECEIVE YOU OUT HERE, AGENT COOL.

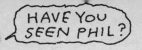 
I start digging in the sand and soon I find a door. Then I find a doorbell. I ring it but nobody answers—so I knock.

"Knock, knock."

"Who's there?" says a voice.

"Irish stew," I answer.

"Irish stew who?" asks the voice.

"Irish stew in the name of the law," I say.

BINGO!

59

The door slowly opens. It's Dr. Gastro.

"All right, Gastro, the beans are up," I declare.

"Who spilled the beans?" he asks.

"It was a half-baked idea," I answer.

"I coulda *bean* a zillionaire," he laments.

"Now you don't amount to a hill of beans."

"I'm a has-*bean*," he says sadly.

"You're outta your bean," I declare.

"You don't know beans," he growls.

"You're full of beans," I smile.

"I don't give a bean," he says.
"Tough beans!" I yell and bean
him.

CHAPTER 16
MISSION ACCOMPLISHED

When I get on the school bus the next morning, no one knows that I saved the world last night. They can't even imagine it. But that's okay. I know it. Being a super spy is a lonely job.

"Hey, what's for lunch today?" asks Eric.

"Probably franks and beans," I say.

"Nothing special about that," he mutters.

"If you only knew," I smile. "If you only knew."

A coded message from Hubie:

20-18-5-1-20
15-20-8-5-18-19
20-8-5
23-1-25
25-15-21-'-4
12-9-11-5
20-8-5-13
20-15
20-18-5-1-20
25-15-21!

(HINT: A=1, B=2, C=3, etc.)